# ONE RED SHOE
## (The Other One's Blue!)

By STEPHANIE CALMENSON

Illustrated by LISA McCUE KARSTEN

A GOLDEN BOOK ● NEW YORK

Western Publishing Company, Inc., Racine, Wisconsin 53404

One morning while Maxine was dressing she said, "Look at my feet, Mommy."

"They are very nice feet," Maxine's mommy said. "Now, why don't you put your shoes on them?"

"Because my toes have something to tell you," said Maxine.

Maxine wiggled her toes wildly.

"Would you ask your toes to speak a little louder?" asked Mrs. Rabbit.

*"We need new shoes!"* said Maxine in her best wiggly-toes voice.

"Well, toes, I can see you have been squeezing into the shoes you have," said Mrs. Rabbit. "So right after breakfast we'll go shopping for new ones."

"Hurray!" cried Maxine's toes.

While her mommy was dressing, Maxine watched
her favorite TV program, *The Spunky Spaniel Show.*
Maxine sang along with Spunky. She knew every word
of his song by heart.

All the way to the shoe store Maxine looked down
at feet.

"Red shoes, green shoes, white shoes, blue shoes.
Wait till they see *my* shoes!" she thought. Then she
asked, "Mommy, may I pick out the color of my new
shoes?"

"I don't see why not," said Mrs. Rabbit.

When they got to the store, Mr. Muskrat greeted them warmly.

"Hi, Mr. Muskrat," said Maxine. "My feet got bigger, so I need new shoes!"

Mr. Muskrat bent down to feel Maxine's toes. They wiggled and wiggled inside her shoes.

"Yes, these feet have grown," said Mr. Muskrat. "Let's see what size they are."

Maxine stepped onto the measuring stick.

"Can you read the number for me, Maxine?" asked
Mr. Muskrat.

"Six!" said Maxine. "Well, almost."

"Now your other foot," said Mr. Muskrat.

"Six again!" said Maxine.

"I'll see what we have in your size," Mr. Muskrat said.

Maxine sang the Spunky Spaniel song while she
waited:

    "Hello, everybody, look at me.

    I'm as spunky as Spunky can be!

    My hat is pink. I have one red shoe.

    But isn't it funny—the other one's blue!"

While she sang she did a little dance.

"Here they are," said Mr. Muskrat. "Red shoes, size six."

Mr. Muskrat put one red shoe on Maxine's foot. But before he could put the other shoe on, Maxine said, "Now I need a blue one."

"Shoes come in pairs," said Mr. Muskrat. "And both shoes in a pair are the same color."

"But Spunky Spaniel has one red shoe and one blue shoe," said Maxine.

"I don't know who Spunky Spaniel is," said Mr.
Muskrat, "but he didn't buy his shoes from me."

"I know you wanted to pick the color," said Mrs.
Rabbit, "but you'll have to choose just one."

While Maxine was deciding her friend Arthur came into the store. He was singing the Spunky Spaniel song, too.

"Hi, Arthur," said Maxine. "What color shoes are you getting?"

"I'm getting one red shoe and one blue," said
Arthur, "just like Spunky Spaniel!"

"You can't do that, because shoes come in pairs,"
Maxine explained. Then she got an idea. "Find out
what size shoe you wear," she whispered to Arthur.

Arthur had his feet measured. "I wear size six," he said.

"Hurray!" said Maxine. "Now if you get blue shoes and I get red, we can share sometimes."

"That's a great idea!" said Arthur.

"I don't think that's going to work, Maxine," said Mr. Muskrat. "You see, Arthur wears alligator size six, and you wear rabbit size six. They are very different sizes."

So Arthur took blue shoes and Maxine took red.
"I wanted to be spunky," said Maxine sadly.
"Me, too," said Arthur.

Maxine and Arthur were starting out of the store when Mr. Muskrat called them back.

"You forgot your gifts," he said. He handed them each a balloon with a small bag tied to the bottom.

"Thank you," said Maxine and Arthur.

When they opened their bags, they both got the same idea.

After a quick switch, Arthur said, "We didn't get to pick the shoes we wanted . . ."

"But these laces are spunky!" said Maxine.
And they danced all the way home—as spunky as
Spunky can be!